HAMSTER PRINCESS

HARRIET the INVINCIBLE

Dial Books for Young Readers
Published by the Penguin Group
Penguin Group (USA) LLC
375 Hudson Street, New York, New York 10014

USA/Canada/UK/Ireland/Australia/New Zealand/India/South Africa/China
PENGUIN.COM
A Penguin Random House Company

Library of Congress Cataloging-in-Publication Data   Vernon, Ursula.
Hamster princess : Harriet the invincible / by Ursula Vernon.   pages cm
Summary: Never a conventional princess, Harriet becomes an adventurer after learning she is cursed
to fall into a deep sleep on her twelfth birthday, but after two years of slaying ogres, cliff-diving, and more
with her riding quail Mumfrey, things go awry at home and she must seek a prince to set things right.
ISBN 978-0-8037-3983-3 (hardcover)
[1. Princesses—Fiction. 2. Adventure and adventurers—Fiction. 3. Blessing and cursing—Fiction.
4. Hamsters—Fiction. 5. Humorous stories.] I. Title.
    PZ7.V5985Ham 2015   [Fic]—dc23   2014034037

Printed in the United States of America
10   9   8   7   6   5   4   3   2   1

Designed by Jennifer Kelly • Text set in Minister Std Light

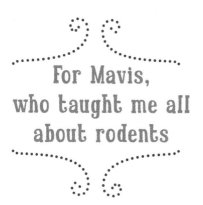

For Mavis,
who taught me all
about rodents

HAMSTER PRINCESS
HARRIET the INVINCIBLE

BY
Ursula Vernon

Dial Books for Young Readers
AN IMPRINT OF PENGUIN
GROUP (USA) LLC

CHAPTER 1

Once upon a time, in a distant land, there was a beautiful princess named Harriet Hamsterbone, who, as her name indicated, was a hamster.

TRUST ME, FOR A HAMSTER, I'M STUNNING.

She was brave and intelligent and excelled in traditional hamster princess skills, like checkers and fractions.

I'VE TAKEN SEVEN-EIGHTHS OF YOUR PIECES. DO YOU WANT TO GIVE UP?

She was not very good at trailing around the palace looking ethereal and sighing a lot, which are also traditional princess skills, but her parents hired deportment teachers to try and make up for it.

Her deportment teacher tried to make her walk around with a book on her head to improve her posture. He was later found in the library with a book stuffed in his mouth, and Harriet was grounded for a month.

She loved her riding quail Mumfrey, and rode him all over the countryside. Riding quail can't actually fly, but they make excellent steeds for hamsters. Harriet and Mumfrey rode everywhere pretending to slay monsters, since her parents would not actually let her go out to slay real dragons. This was a source of great disappointment for her.

Despite being kept away from monsters, Harriet was generally happy and not as irritating as some princesses. Yet her mom and dad were often depressed, for they knew that a dark cloud hung over the princess, and indeed, the very kingdom.

For when the princess was only twelve days old, on the day she was to be christened, a dreadful curse had been placed upon her, and despite their best efforts, the hamster king and queen had no idea how to break it.

CHAPTER 2

The Christening: Ten Years Earlier

On the day of the princess's christening, everyone in the palace and many of the most important people in the kingdom had come out to witness the ceremony.

No expense had been spared. In the usual Hamsterbone tradition, there were dukes and earls and a marquess, which is something like a marquis, and several viscounts and one regular count and even a praetor. (The praetor had taken a wrong turn some weeks ago while hunting. He didn't know what the hamsters were talking about, but had heard something about free food. Praetors are elected officials in certain kinds of kingdoms, and they never pass up free meals.)

And of course there were three fairy god-mice, to administer the blessings, and the princess herself.

OKAY. WE'VE GOT THE THREE FAIRY GOD-MICE, WE'VE GOT THE PRINCESS... AM I FORGETTING SOMETHING?

DID YOU INVITE THE WICKED FAIRY GOD-MOUSE?

WHY WOULD I INVITE A *WICKED* FAIRY TO OUR DAUGHTER'S CHRISTENING?

The assembled crowd shrank back when the wicked fairy appeared, for it was immediately obvious to all that this was no ordinary fairy, but in fact the wicked Ratshade, who had placed third on *Fairy God-Mouse Today*'s Most Wicked List for eleven years running. Rumor had it that she was a bit bitter about her inability to move up the list, and had been planning something big.

Ratshade was tall and thin, and her fingernails were so long that they curved in strange rippling claws and made it very difficult for her to blow her nose without causing herself serious injury. Her fur was as white as bone, her eyes were red, and she had a stump for a tail, because she had traded her tail for power when she was young. (This is a thing that rats can do, although most of them are very attached to their tails and wouldn't dream of parting with them.)

Ratshade stomped across the dais toward the bassinet that contained the princess. Two fairy god-mice cowered back, but the youngest clutched the back of the bassinet, prepared to snatch the princess away if Ratshade tried to grab her.

But Ratshade did not touch the princess. She only gazed down at her, clicking her long nails together, and then she laughed, a laugh like bones clattering down a hole in the dark.

"Very well!" said the wicked fairy. "Very well! She is twelve days old today? Well, when she is twelve *years* old, she shall prick her finger upon a hamster wheel and fall into a sleep like death!"

Ratshade vanished in a cloud of oily smoke that smelled like burning hair, and the inhabitants of the kingdom looked at one another in dismay. The princess was cursed!

CHAPTER 3

What can we possibly do?" cried the dukes.

"There's nothing we can do!" cried the earls.

"Very difficult to break, fairy curses," said the marquess.

"They come true no matter what," said the viscounts.

"They'll bend the world around them and *make* themselves come true," said the regular count.

"Maybe the other fairies can do something," said the praetor, helping himself to the buffet.

Everyone stared at him.

WHAT?

"Brilliant!" cried the dukes and the earls and the marquess and the viscounts and the regular count. "We never would have thought of that!"

"I can't believe my empire never conquered yours when we had the chance," muttered the praetor into his sandwich.

So the three fairy god-mice put their heads together, while the hamster queen tried to comfort the princess, who had slept through the entire thing and did not actually need comforting.

"Right!" said the oldest of the fairy god-mice. "We cannot break Ratshade's curse, O King Hamsterbone, but we can alter it a little. I have changed the curse so that when the princess falls asleep, she shall not need either food or drink while she is sleeping."

"I guess that's useful," said the queen.

"What about bathrooms?" asked the king. "I mean, I always have to get up in the middle of the night to use the toilet, so—"

"No bathrooms either," said the oldest fairy god-mouse, and gave the king a very stern look.

"And I," said the middle god-mouse, "have changed the curse so that at the moment it takes effect, enormous thorny briars shall grow up around the princess's tower, so that no one can get in."

"Um," said the king. "That . . . doesn't sound *quite* so useful."

OR VERY GOOD FOR OUR PROPERTY VALUES.

"Tough," said the middle fairy god-mouse, annoyed. "It's already cast."

The hamster king and queen sighed, and turned to the third god-mouse without much hope.

"So what did you do?" asked the king. "Set the

palace on fire? Turn her into a snowflake or a chicken or something?"

"Errr . . . no," said the youngest god-mouse. "I don't do chickens." She looked down at her feet. "I don't know if mine will be very useful."

"Out with it," said the king.

I, UM, CHANGED THE CURSE SO THAT THE KISS OF A PRINCE WILL WAKE HER.

"Wonderful!" cried the dukes, earls, marquess, viscounts, and regular count. (The praetor had filled his pockets with sandwiches and gone back to his own country.)

"Now that's fairy work!" said the king admiringly.

"Ideally I'd like her to get to know the prince a bit before he kisses her," said the queen. "Make sure he's a nice boy and understands how to treat his mother-in-law. But that's still a very good change, my dear!" She beamed at the youngest fairy god-mouse, who looked embarrassed by all the attention.

And so the princess was christened, and the curse was cast.

CHAPTER 4

Despite the doom upon her, Princess Harriet grew up happy. Her parents tried not to worry about the curse, but of course it was difficult. Even though there were a number of princes around that might be convinced to kiss an enchanted princess, the king and queen fretted.

Princes were not always reliable, and of course they tended not to show up until after the fact. And what if the god-mice hadn't done their jobs correctly?

No one knew where to find the wicked fairy Ratshade, who was the only one who might be able to take the curse off completely.

Hamster wheels were banned from the palace grounds completely, but it was impossible to burn every wheel in the kingdom. Hamsters love their wheels. The king's advisors told him that it was either the curse or a peasant uprising, and since the curse would find a way to happen *anyway*, he was better off leaving the wheels alone.

To make matters worse, Harriet herself grew increasingly bored with life in the palace, and kept wanting to take up more dangerous hobbies.

PRINCESSES DO NOT GO CLIFF-DIVING!

Finally, when she was ten years old and the time of the curse was only two years away, her parents took her aside and told her the entire story of the curse.

Harriet's parents watched her closely to see how she was taking the news. She sat on the floor and chewed thoughtfully on her lower lip for a while.

"Okay . . . let me get this straight . . ." she said finally.

"Yes, dear?" said the queen.

"So I'm going to prick myself on a hamster wheel on my twelfth birthday and fall asleep, possibly forever, or at least until a prince kisses me." Harriet's tone left it very clear that she didn't put much faith in princes.

"Right," said the king.

AND THIS IS GOING TO HAPPEN NO MATTER WHAT.

"Fairy curses are very persistent, dear," said her mother. "You can't thwart them. We did try."

"The fairies were very clear on that," said her father gloomily. "Even if we locked you in a room and didn't let anyone in, on your twelfth birthday, a hamster wheel would show up somehow."

"Ratshade is the only one who can change it," said the queen, "and she's vanished completely. She didn't even make the *Fairy God-Mouse Today* Most Wicked List last year."

BUT THIS IS *WONDERFUL!*

WHEEEEE!

Princess Harriet celebrated her newfound freedom by jumping from the top of the highest tower in the kingdom into the moat. She survived three jumps and a belly-flop, because the curse did indeed have to keep her alive until her twelfth birthday. Wicked fairies put a lot of work into their curses, and they hate to see them thwarted by unfortunate accidents.

And so Princess Harriet spent the next two years cliff-diving, dragon-slaying, and jousting on the professional circuit.

SHE PULLED A SWORD FROM A STONE. APPARENTLY THERE'S BEEN SOME CONFUSION. THEY MADE HER PUT IT BACK.

"At least she's not still visiting with that awful Crone of the Blighted Waste," said the king. "She didn't sound very nice at all."

"Harriet wrote that she made good cookies."

The princess always wrote home regularly. Her mother would have been appalled to know what she was leaving out of the letters. Just recently, she had decided to Do Something about the people-eating Ogrecats, which had been such a scourge up and down the coast.

Her mother wouldn't have approved at all, so she just said that she was going to the beach.

"I keep thinking we should put a stop to this," said the king sadly, "but she has so little time left to have fun."

"I know," said the queen. No one had been able to find Ratshade, and there were only three months left before Harriet's twelfth birthday.

CHAPTER 5

Harriet, meanwhile, was having the time of her life. She could go anywhere! Do anything! Climb the highest mountain! Jump off the tallest cliff! The curse wouldn't even let her drown, which allowed her to go underwater and talk to mer-hamsters, although she had to leave Mumfrey on shore and he got into a bit of a snit about it.

HMMPH!

That evening, in the desolate and dreary Swamp of Sorrow (formerly the Bog of Bleariness, formerly the Fen of Fear, formerly the Marsh of Misery, formerly Farmer Bob's Mud and Cattail Farm, Inc.), Princess Harriet composed a letter home.

Princess Harriet studied the letter. No, "Dreaded Ogrecat" would only worry her mother. Perhaps she'd say she was trying to find the Relatively Pleasant Fluffycat of Olingsturm . . . although that didn't make it any easier to spell . . .

She decided to write the rest of the letter later, when she had access to a dictionary, or perhaps an atlas. She put her pen away. Anyway, it wasn't time to write letters. It was time to sleep, and then tomorrow morning, it would be time to pull out her sword and fight monsters.

CHAPTER 6

The Ogrecat left enormous paw prints in the muck. They were easy to follow, even with the gloom and the mist that kept oozing around the ground in the Swamp of Sorrow.

"This is the last ogre of the trip, Mumfrey," Princess Harriet said to her faithful riding quail.

"Then we'll head home to the palace. It's a long way home, and Mom will never forgive me if I turn twelve and fall into a horrible enchanted sleep without her."

"Qwerrrrk," agreed Mumfrey.

Several hours later, they finally arrived at the Ogrecat's den. The Ogrecat himself was enormous, with long fangs and bright green eyes and whiskers as thick as drinking straws.

He was squinting at a very small book held in the tips of his claws.

"Perfect!" whispered Harriet. "You know what to do, Mumfrey. On the count of three . . ."

"Qwerk . . ." cheeped Mumfrey. ". . . querrk . . . QWERRRK!"

"What the—" said the Ogrecat, dropping his book as a small, ferocious hamster landed on him.

"DIE, FOUL BEAST!" screamed Harriet.

"QWERRRRRK!" screamed Mumfrey.

"OWWWW!" screamed the Ogrecat.

PECK!
PECK!
PECK!

"Your days of eating people are through, you monster!" cried Harriet. The Ogrecat flung her off with a wild shake of his arms and the hamster princess soared through the air, did a reverse one-handed cartwheel (the other hand was holding the sword), and shot to her feet. "You'll rue the day that Princess Harriet heard of your evil ways!"

She couldn't reach much higher than his knees, so she brought the hilt of her sword down on his toes. He yelped.

"Time-out!" shrieked the Ogrecat, hopping on one foot and trying to pry Mumfrey off his head. "Time-out, time-out, *time-out!*"

"Monsters generally aren't allowed to call time-outs," said Harriet, stepping back, "but I suppose I'll allow it. You have to put Mumfrey back on your head afterward though, or it isn't fair."

"Fine!" said the Ogrecat. "I'll put him anywhere you like! Just get him off and stop hitting me!"

"You heard the Ogre, Mumfrey," said Harriet. "Let him go. At least temporarily." She glared at the Ogrecat.

Mumfrey sniffed haughtily and stepped down from the Ogrecat's head. He liked fighting monsters. It was much more interesting than roosting in the palace stables all day, like the other quail back home, and he was disappointed that he had to stop.

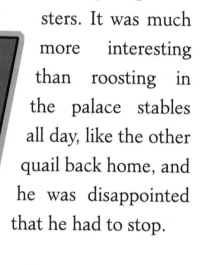

SNIFF

"You're *Harriet*," said the Ogrecat, sounding as if he had just gotten smallpox for Christmas.

"*Princess* Harriet," said the hamster princess. "You've heard of me?"

"We've *all* heard of you," said the Ogrecat. "All the ogres, anyway. Crazy Princess Harriet, and her mad fighting quail."

Mumfrey beamed as much as you can beam with a beak.

QWERK!

CRAZY? WHO ARE YOU CALLING CRAZY?

"You're a princess," said the Ogrecat. "You jump on monsters in the middle of the swamp and beat them senseless. For a princess, that's pretty crazy."

"I got bored with deportment lessons," said Harriet, annoyed. "Is that all this is? Because I'm a princess, and if I'm beating monsters senseless, it is something that princesses do, okay? And anyway, *you* eat people, so I don't think you get to tell me how to live."

"I don't eat people," said the Ogrecat. "Not anymore. Haven't for months now."

YOU DON'T?

"If you heard that a crazy hamster princess with a sword was attacking ogres who ate people, wouldn't *you* consider a change of diet?"

Harriet thought about this. It did seem logical, and it was cool that her reputation had spread so far, but it was a bit disappointing to come all this way and discover that the monster had already gone on a diet. "So what do you eat?"

"Soy, mostly," said the Ogrecat. "They do a pretty good person-flavored tofu. Of course, the texture's not quite right, but everybody heard what you did to my great-aunt, so I can live with the texture." He rooted around until he found the book he had dropped, which was titled *To Serve Man-Flavored Substitute*, and waved it at her. Apparently it was a cookbook.

"Which one was your great-aunt?" asked Harriet, who had not previously considered that the various ogres might be related.

THE SWIMMING OGRECAT OF THE BARNACLE COAST.

OH, *HER.* YEAH, OKAY, I REMEMBER.

IT TOOK HER
THREE DAYS TO GET THE
LOBSTER OUT OF HER EAR.
THEY HAD TO USE
PLIERS.

Princess Harriet wandered around the Ogrecat's front yard. Unlike the front yards of some previous ogres, there were not piles of bones lying around. There *was* a skull hanging over the front door, but it looked old, and it was wearing a jaunty hat.

"About that skull—" she began.

"Traveling salesman," said the ogre. "He tried to sell me non-stick cookware. And that was twenty-six years ago, so give me a break."

Princess Harriet had to admit that the statute of limitations on eating traveling non-stick cookware salesmen had probably elapsed after twenty-six years. She wandered around the yard some more.

"Soy, huh?"

"Mostly. Some chickpeas. I could make hummus, if you're hungry." The ogre waved his claws. "I have kale chips?"

Harriet shuddered. Kale chips were a foe beyond any hero's strength.

"So I guess I don't need to beat you up, then," she said.

"I'd really prefer you didn't."

"Qwerk!"

The ogre made very good hot tea and even had a saucer for Mumfrey. It was all very cozy. Since the last time Harriet had spent any time with an ogre, it was trying to eat her, it felt a little weird.

"Qwerk," said Mumfrey, which was Quail for
"Yeah, but what're you gonna do?"

"I guess that's all the ogres, though," said Harriet.

"Qwerk," agreed Mumfrey.

The hamster princess sighed. "So that's it, then. Time to go home . . ."

CHAPTER 7

The day that Princess Harriet was to return home, the entire court assembled in the great hall. Everyone came out, including the dukes, the earls, the viscounts, and the regular count (the marquess was home with measles), as well as various servants and staff and hangers-on and a special guest.

They waited in the great hall for three hours, until everyone was thoroughly bored and had to go to the bathroom, and then a servant rushed in and whispered something in the hamster queen's ear.

"What?" said the queen. "In her *room?*"

Apparently Princess Harriet had arrived very early, gone directly to the stables to make sure that Mumfrey had all the birdseed he could eat, and then went to her bedroom and went to bed.

"Go wake her up!" yelled the queen.

The queen went up the ninety-six stairs to Harriet's tower. It was a lot of stairs to climb, so the princess had marked every stair with a fraction to let you know how far up the stairs you were.

The hamster queen was panting by the time she reached the top, and reconsidering the wisdom of putting Harriet's bedroom at the top of a high tower, but princesses lived in towers. It was traditional.

"Harriet?" she said, pushing the door open. "Honey, are you home?"

Princess Harriet was indeed home. She was also snoring loudly enough to rattle the windowpanes, and clutching her sword in her sleep.

The queen sighed and shook Harriet's shoulder. "Honey, it's time to get up."

"Hrrgggggkkkk . . ." said Harriet.

The queen tried again. "Honey . . ."

"Znnggghk!"

There is a power that all mothers possess, although some of them rarely use it, to wake their children from a profound sleep. Queen Hamsterbone gritted her teeth, took a deep breath, and yelled:

IT'S TIME TO GET UP!

Harriet shot out of bed with her sword, swung it wildly over her head, realized that it was her mother, and dropped the sword on her own foot.

"Yerowrch!"

"Oh good," said the hamster queen, adjusting her skirts. "You're awake."

Harriet picked up her sword and rubbed her smarting toes. She felt a sudden sympathy for the Ogrecat of Olingsturm.

"You need to get dressed," said the queen. "The court is waiting for you!"

"Court?" asked Harriet blearily. "What court? I haven't been arrested. I don't need to go to court. They can't prove anything. I was nowhere near that chicken. I demand a lawyer!"

"The *royal* court," said her mother patiently. "The dukes and the earls and the viscounts and—"

OH. THEM.

NOW, NOW. THEY'RE ALL VERY EAGER TO WELCOME YOU HOME.

THEN THEY SHOULD HAVE BEEN HERE AT FOUR THIS MORNING.

"I don't know what you were thinking, traveling at such a beastly hour," said the queen, while Harriet tried to make her clothes look as if she hadn't slept in them.

"Mumfrey was homesick," said the princess. "It took longer to get home than I thought it would."

"I should say so!" The queen folded her arms. "Do you know that it's only a week until your birthday? It's hardly enough time to get your dress sewn and the cake baked and the musicians brought in and—"

"The army of gardeners with pruning shears," muttered Harriet, who remembered the part of the curse about the brambles.

The queen frowned.

"Mom," said Harriet, "there's no point in pretending that this is a normal birthday. You'd be better off skipping the musicians and hiring every fairy in the land to try and fend off Ratshade."

CHAPTER 8

The week before Harriet's birthday passed very quickly for everyone except Harriet.

The dukes, the earls, the viscounts, and the regular count wished her a happy upcoming birthday at least five times a day. This got old quickly.

The queen refused to talk about Ratshade or hamster wheels, and would turn the conversation immediately to whether the cake should be chocolate or carrot.

The king, meanwhile . . .

"He means well," Harriet told Mumfrey one evening. "It's just that he does it five or six times a day. And I keep running into him because he's pacing around my bedroom tower muttering about brambles and the foundations. He even ordered two hundred gallons of weed-killer, but Mom made him get rid of it because it wasn't organic."

"Qwerk," said Mumfrey.

"But at least he's thinking about it! Mom keeps changing the subject. If I have to hear about fabric swatches and puffed sleeves one more time, I'm going to go *find* Ratshade and *throw* myself on the stupid hamster wheel, just to make it *stop!*"

"Qwerk," agreed Mumfrey, pecking birdseed out of her hand.

"And as for Prince Cecil . . ." She shuddered.

It is not entirely fair to say that Harriet disliked

Prince Cecil on sight, because she actually disliked him before they ever met, thanks to her mother.

But it's fair to say that meeting Prince Cecil did not make her any happier.

He did not like riding quail or fighting monsters. He kept trying to explain things to her—things she already knew perfectly well, like how to play checkers and how to reduce a fraction to the lowest common denominator.

And he seemed to think that she ought to be grateful he was willing to kiss her.

"I'm *not* going to marry him," said Harriet. "I beat him three times at checkers and he had the gall to tell me I was getting better at the game, like I haven't been playing since I was a little kid! Can you imagine being married to that?"

Mumfrey shrugged.

"I'll run away and become a traveling monster-slayer first. I'll paint my shield black and wear black armor and call myself the Black Knight and people will go 'Ooooh, she's so mysterious . . .'"

"Qwerk!" said Mumfrey, which meant "Uh-huh."

"We'll dye your feathers black too."

"QWERK!"

"Oh, well," said Harriet, sighing. "My birthday's tomorrow, anyway. At least it'll finally be over. I'm almost looking forward to the deathly sleep, just so I get a rest."

Q-W-E-R-R-K . . .

IT'S OKAY, MUMFREY. THEY'LL FIND A WAY TO BREAK THE CURSE.

She wasn't that worried about the curse. At least stupid Prince Cecil ought to be good for that. She was mostly worried about Mumfrey, who would pine away if she spent more than a few days asleep. She'd already made the stable-master promise to come and read him bedtime stories, and to make sure he got extra grain in the evenings.

Besides, there was a whole squadron of armed guards waiting for her up in the tower. Once she was done saying good-bye to Mumfrey in the sta-ble, she was going to be under guard from dawn until dusk.

Harriet sighed, petted Mumfrey's beak, and turned away, whereupon she ran into a tall, bony white rat with angry red eyes.

"Sorry," said Harriet automatically, "I . . . didn't . . . see you . . ."

"Qweeeerrk," said Mumfrey, and kicked the door of his stall nervously.

Her gaze went slowly over the rat, from the bone-white fur to the stump of a tail.

YOU'RE *RATSHADE!*

ndeed I am," said Ratshade. "Indeed, in-very-deed." She glared down at Harriet.

Twelve years had not changed Ratshade. She looked as pale and hungry and evil as ever, although her claws were much shorter.

EVERYBODY SAID YOU HAD REALLY LONG CLAWS, THOUGH.

I'M GETTING OVER A BAD HEAD-COLD. THEY KEPT GOING THROUGH THE TISSUES. IT'S A PAIN, BECAUS THEY GROW SO FAST AND I HAVE TO KEEP CLIPPING THEM, AND— LOOK, CAN WE GET THIS OVER WITH?

"But it's not my birthday yet," said Harriet. She wasn't as frightened as she should have been. She'd spent years fighting ogres ten times the size of Ratshade. She did wish that she had her sword, but her mother had confiscated it after the deportment teacher had shown up with another book to balance on her head and Harriet had chopped the book into pieces.

"Yes, it is," said Ratshade. "Your birthday is on the seventeenth of August."

"No, the eighteenth," said Harriet.

IT'S THE SEVENTEENTH. YOUR FATHER THE KING IS VERY BAD WITH DATES, AND YOUR MOTHER WAS KIND OF OCCUPIED WITH HAVING A BABY.

Harriet was forced to admit that this was entirely possible. Her father was one of those people who was always wandering into a room and asking "What day is it? Is it Tuesday?" when it was actually Saturday, and had once famously misplaced the entire month of November.

"Huh," said Harriet. "So it's my birthday today. And here you are."

"And here I am," agreed Ratshade.

There was an awkward silence. Harriet stuffed her hands in her pockets.

83

"I can't help but notice you aren't begging for mercy," said Ratshade.

"Not really my style," said Harriet apologetically. "Sorry."

"Not a lot of weeping either."

"I don't weep," said Harriet. "Every now and then I have a good cry, but weeping isn't my thing. And I'm not going to swoon either, so don't bother."

"Hmph!" Ratshade folded her arms. "Not very *princessly*, are you?"

HAVE YOU BEEN TALKING TO MY MOTHER? WEREN'T YOU THE ONE WHO WANTED TO GET THIS OVER WITH?

"Fine," grumbled Ratshade. "It's just not very satisfactory, cursing a princess and then when you show up, the princess is in the stable—"

"Qwerk!" snapped Mumfrey, and kicked his stall door again.

"—and she's not begging for mercy or anything. Do you know how hard that curse was? And then I had to go into hiding for *years* so that nobody could find me and force me to break it."

"Yes, yes," said Harriet, who was already getting tired of talking to Ratshade. "I'm sure it's been awful. Now where's the hamster wheel?"

"In the stableyard," said Ratshade sulkily.

Harriet followed the wicked fairy out of the stable and into the broad open yard where the quail exercised during the day. Mumfrey, who was quite intelligent for a quail (which admittedly is sort of like being intelligent for a grapefruit), gathered himself up and jumped over the stall door so that he could accompany his rider to her fate.

"Aww," said Harriet, patting the quail's neck. "You're a good boy, Mumfrey."

"Qwerk," grumbled Mumfrey, which was Quail for "I want to kick that rat in the face."

Princess Harriet stepped into the stableyard, and beheld her doom.

CHAPTER 10

In her travels across the land, jousting and jumping off high objects, Princess Harriet had encountered any number of wheels. Hamster wheels were very popular across the kingdom. Hamsters ran on them for exercise, for fun, and more importantly, to power things like flour mills and forges and cooking spits and anything else where you needed a lot of rotary motion and didn't have a windmill or a watermill available.

She had never actually used one, however, because while she wasn't afraid of the curse, she also wasn't stupid.

Even if she had been fond of hamster wheels, she probably wouldn't have used this one. It was old and rusted and had sharp pointy bits of metal sticking off it and enormous jagged splinters and little tiny hard-to-see splinters, the sort that get into your foot and require someone with tweezers and a needle to get it back out again.

"Yeesh," said Harriet.

"Qwerrrrk..." said Mumfrey.

"Well, there it is," said Ratshade grumpily. "One hamster wheel. Go jab yourself on it, and we'll get this over with. If I start work now, I might be able to make *Fairy God-Mouse Today*'s Most Wicked List this year."

Harriet stared at the wheel, her mind working furiously, and then turned back to Ratshade.

"Before I do—"

WANT TO BEG FOR MERCY *NOW?* IT'S A BIT LATE.

"No, no," said Harriet. "Actually, I wanted to thank you."

Ratshade immediately looked deeply suspicious. People did not usually thank wicked fairies. The mouse who delivered her groceries often said, "Here you go, ma'am, thank you for not killing me," but you couldn't really count that.

IT WAS YOUR CURSE THAT MADE ME INVINCIBLE.

THE CURSE HAD TO KEEP ME ALIVE, SO I WAS ABLE TO GO OUT AND FIGHT MONSTERS AND LEARN TO CLIFF-DIVE AND GO JOUSTING, AND DO ALL KINDS OF THINGS THAT PRINCESSES DON'T GET TO DO.

Ratshade did not have eyebrows, but she had big pokey whiskers that went up in surprise. "Really?"

"Yeah," said Harriet. "I've had a really good life, because of your curse. I got to do all kinds of stuff." She took a step toward Ratshade. "So— well, I couldn't shake your hand before, probably, but since you've trimmed your claws . . ."

She stuck out her hand.

"Oh . . . well . . ." Ratshade felt completely out of her depth now. She was a wicked fairy. She knew how this was supposed to go. A normal princess would be weeping and swooning and falling down, and then Ratshade would press her hand against the wheel—or if the princess was a real numb-skull, she'd go "Oh! A hamster wheel!" and run up to it herself, which was practically shooting fish in a barrel—and then the curse would take and everybody could get on with their lives.

This was *not* a normal princess.

Ratshade felt vaguely embarrassed and determined to get this over with as quickly as possible. "Right. Um. You're welcome, I guess." She reached out to shake Harriet's hand.

Harriet grinned.

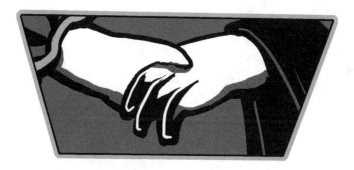

Just being invincible doesn't make you good with a sword. Swinging swords is an art form. Harriet didn't have a sword with her, but she still had the muscles she'd earned from two years of riding around and swinging swords at people, and now she had Ratshade's hand.

"Whaaaat?!" yelled the wicked fairy as Harriet whipped her around and charged toward the hamster wheel.

Now, there are any number of things that a wicked fairy can do to stop someone who is attacking her. Ratshade could have put Harriet to sleep or set her on fire or turned her into a sack of turnips, all without breaking a sweat.

All of those things, however, require at least a second or two and a couple of magic words to pull off.

She didn't get a second or two.

Harriet slammed her into the hamster wheel, hard enough to give the wicked fairy a shoulder full of splinters.

The curse took.

The princess *felt* it take, a great wash of cold air that ruffled her fur and pinned her ears back. Someone had pricked themselves on the enchanted wheel ... but it was the wrong person.

Ratshade screamed.

Sparks arced and cracked over the rat's fur and between her whiskers. The smell of burning hair made Harriet's eyes water. The hamster dropped the wicked fairy and staggered backward into Mumfrey.

The cold wind grew stronger and seemed to blow out of the wheel, whipping past them. Mumfrey dug his claws into the ground to keep from being knocked off his feet.

The cold wind whipped around them once, twice, three times—and the third time knocked Harriet into Mumfrey and knocked Mumfrey into the stable wall.

And then there was silence.

CHAPTER 11

Princess Harriet got to her feet.

After a moment or two, so did Mumfrey, although he was missing a couple of feathers.

The stableyard, strangely enough, did not look as if a magical cyclone had whipped through it. The haystacks were still in their mounds, not blown halfway across the kingdom. A cricket chirped somewhere in the stillness, then thought better of it, and didn't chirp again.

The one thing that clearly *had* been hit by the magic wind was the enchanted hamster wheel. The frame was broken into a hundred pieces. It looked like a pile of kindling, not like the bringer of a terrible fairy curse.

Ratshade lay atop the pile, her eyes closed.

"Uh-oh," said Harriet. "Is she dead?" You didn't generally get in trouble for killing wicked fairies, but fairies are still people, and she felt a little funny about it.

Mumfrey was trying to preen his wings to cover the bare patches where his missing feathers had been. He gave Ratshade an unfriendly look.

Harriet didn't want to get close enough to the pile of wood to poke her, just in case the curse was still active. It wouldn't have been possible to climb the pile without getting at least *one* splinter.

Fortunately, at that moment Ratshade snored.

"She's asleep," said Harriet, with a sigh of relief. "The curse backfired on her. Whew."

MAN,
MOM AND DAD
ARE GONNA BE *SO*
HAPPY . . .

Another sound came to her attention then.

It was not quite a rustling and not quite a creaking and there was almost a hissing, but also a groaning—what was it? Harriet had never heard anything quite like it.

She turned around and around the stableyard, trying to figure out where it was coming from. She had just about decided that it was coming from all directions and was thinking that she *really* wanted her sword—and then she saw it.

The brambles were growing.

It was really no wonder that Harriet didn't recognize the sound. Very few people on earth have ever heard the sound of a plant growing at a thousand times the normal speed. (The middle fairy god-mouse would have recognized it, of course, but she had given up god-mousing some years earlier and had started a lucrative career selling organic cabbages.)

The brambles shot up around the palace walls like flailing serpents, great whippy vines of green and brown, coiling around the base of the tower and slithering over the stable roof.

For a minute, Harriet thought that they might actually overgrow the stableyard and that she and Mumfrey were going to have to run for it, but the vines stopped at the edges as if they'd run into a wall. They waved back and forth, putting out thorns as long as a dragon's claws, then hurriedly

grew upward, arcing overhead and weaving together until it looked as if a giant wicker basket
had been dropped over the top of the palace.

The stones of the palace creaked in protest as
vines scrabbled and clawed at them.

Harriet remembered how her father had fretted over the impact of fast-growing brambles on the foundations of the tower. This ... this was impacting a bit more than the tower.

"I guess we should go tell them I beat Ratshade," said Harriet. "They're bound to have noticed the plants by now, anyway." She cast a last glimpse up at the bramble roof, and saw a star winking at her through a gap in the thorns.

CHAPTER 12

It turned out to be a bit more complicated than that.

Harriet first noticed the problem when she went back into the stable. All the quail were asleep with their wings over their heads. Well, it was evening, that wasn't unusual, but they didn't wake up, not even when Harriet rattled the birdseed bin getting Mumfrey his dinner.

Normally the sound of the birdseed bin would bring all the quail in the stable to high alert.

The head stablehand was asleep in the corner of one of the stalls, leaning up against the wall, and he didn't wake up when Harriet talked to him.

Princess Harriet was starting to get a sinking feeling in her stomach.

She hurried across the little alley that separated the stables from the main palace. Thorns meshed overhead. When she pulled the door open, the guard who had been leaning against the door fell down in front of her with a clatter of armor . . . and he didn't wake up either.

The butler was asleep. The maids were asleep. In the great hall, the dukes and the earls and the viscounts and the regular count were all asleep at the dining table, and the servants who were bringing them food had lain down on the floor and were sleeping curled around their serving trays. Prince Cecil was sprawled out, face-down.

And worst of all, at the far end of the hall, curled up in the seat of the enormous thrones...

Everyone in the palace was asleep, except for Harriet and Mumfrey. She ran up to the top of the tower and down to the depths of the wine cellar, and every person she found was sleeping. In the royal kennels, even the fierce hunting newts were sleeping in soggy piles, making wet, snuffly little snores.

There were, as it happened, one hundred seventeen people in the palace at that time (not including quail and newts) and Harriet, who had a mathematical turn of mind, counted all of them to make sure that every single one was actually present and asleep.

117, AND I'VE FOUND 33, SO THAT'S 33/117, WHICH REDUCES TO 11/39, WHICH ... DOESN'T REDUCE ANY FURTHER. BETTER GO FIND MORE PEOPLE.

They were all there.

She had a hopeful few minutes when she couldn't find one hundred fifteen and one hundred sixteen, but it turned out that they were both in the boys' bathroom, where she initially hadn't thought to look. (And which was very dirty compared to the girls' bathroom. Harriet did not stay long.)

She herself was number one hundred seventeen, and with the addition of Ratshade, that meant that she and Mumfrey were the only ones awake in a palace of one hundred eighteen people.

One over one hundred eighteen was a very, very small fraction.

When she tried to wake them up, nothing happened. She poked the dukes and yelled at the earls and sang "Wakey-wakey!" to the viscounts and rolled Prince Cecil down a short flight of steps (he probably deserved it) and none of them even stopped snoring.

THIS IS NOT ENCOURAGING.

Eventually she went back to Mumfrey, because there is something very, very creepy about being the only person awake in an enchanted palace. Everyone in the stable was asleep too, including all the other quail, but at least she didn't have to look at them, and quail don't really snore.

OKAY, MUMFREY. I THINK WE'RE IN TROUBLE.

QWERK?

BUT WE'LL GET THROUGH THIS. TOMORROW MORNING, WE'LL HACK OUR WAY OUT OF THE BRAMBLES AND THEN WE'LL GO FIND SOMEONE WHO CAN HELP US.

QWERRRRKK?

THE ONLY PERSON WHO MIGHT KNOW. WE'RE GOING TO VISIT THE CRONE OF THE BLIGHTED WASTE.

CHAPTER 13

The Crone of the Blighted Waste had what is possibly the least accurate name in the history of magical rodents.

When someone says *crone,* you will likely think of someone like Ratshade—withered and cruel, with a long pointy nose and warts tucked in unusual places. What you might not know is that *crone* is a courtesy title among witches, and means that you are very good at magic indeed.

The Crone of the Blighted Waste was a plump,

motherly guinea pig who always had fresh cookies available. And the Blighted Waste itself, while it had been very blighted and very unpleasant several centuries ago, had been turned into affordable senior housing years earlier, so the crone lived off to one side of a rather nice park with lots of flowers.

Princess Harriet rode up to the crone's door, slid off Mumfrey's back, and rang the doorbell.

The crone opened it, looked down at the bedraggled princess, and said, "Good heavens! You look like you've been dragged backward through a briar patch!"

IT WAS FRONTWARD, ACTUALLY. I HAD TO HACK MY WAY THROUGH. IT TOOK EVERY AX IN THE CASTLE, TWO SWORDS, AND A COUPLE OF MEAT CLEAVERS. I'M VERY TIRED.

COME IN AND HAVE SOME COOKIES.

The crone bustled around the house, getting cookies and, being a thoughtful witch, also brought Band-Aids and some nasty-smelling gunk in a bottle. "Hold still," she told Harriet, applying the gunk to the princess's scratches.

"Ow," said Harriet. It stung, as almost all nasty-smelling gunk does.

"It'll keep them from getting infected," said the crone. "You're no longer invincible now, you know, and you will have to start getting used to it."

Harriet sighed. She'd been trying not to think about it. If the curse was off, that meant that her magical invulnerability was also gone. She might even have to give up cliff-diving.

"So you can tell the curse is gone?" she asked, taking a cookie.

The crone laughed. "My dear, every fairy in a fifty-mile radius felt *that* curse go. What on earth did you do to poor Ratshade?"

"Threw her into the enchanted hamster wheel. And you don't get to feel sorry for her! She's the *wicked* fairy!"

"My dear," said the crone, passing a cookie out the open window to Mumfrey, "I would feel sorry for *anyone* who went up against you. When did we first meet? That poor giant, wasn't it?"

"Yup," said Harriet. "He had that awful Jack fellow bothering him."

"Nasty fellow," said the crone, shuddering. "Chopping down his vegetables and stealing the silverware. I had to make all those traps."

"The traps worked," said Harriet. "All I had to do was drag him out after he'd gotten stuck."

"Right," said the crone. "You did very well. And

so, as long as I have known you, my dear, you have been tough and stubborn and inclined to bull-doze everything in your path."

"So I am allowed to feel a *little* sorry for Rat-shade, who clearly did not know what she was up against." She took a sip of tea.

THREW HER INTO HER OWN ENCHANTED WHEEL! HEE-HEE! DEAR ME!

"What I don't understand," said Harriet, helping herself to another cookie, "is why I didn't fall asleep. Everyone else in the palace is out like a light, except for me and Mumfrey."

"Oh, that's simple enough," said the crone. "When magic backfires on its wielder like that, you get a—a magical tornado of sorts. A cyclone, if you will. And in the very center of a tornado or a cyclone, you have the eye of the storm, which is a completely calm place. I suspect that you and your darling little quail—"

"Qwerk!" said Mumfrey, who was not willing to be called a darling little quail, even by someone who kept handing him cookies.

"—I'm sorry, your big, fierce, *heroic* quail—"

"Qwerk," said Mumfrey, pleased.

"—were fortunate enough to be in the eye of the magical storm. Since you were the one to deal with Ratshade, you could hardly have avoided it. Once everyone was asleep, of course, the modifications to the spell took effect. I suspect that none of your people will have to eat or drink while they are asleep, and the brambles seem to have grown around the entire palace quite nicely."

Harriet sat and thought about this. This was heavy thinking, and required several more cookies and another cup of tea.

CHAPTER 14

"Fortunately for you," said the Crone of the Blighted Waste, "the same prince ought to do it. I don't think you'll have to find—what is it—one hundred and seventeen new princes? Plus however many for the quail. That would be quite daunting."

Harriet groaned. The thought of *one* prince was daunting. Prince Cecil had been . . . well, pretty awful. Finding another prince to kiss him . . .

She groaned again, with feeling.

THEY *WILL* HAVE TO KISS EVERYONE UNDER THE SPELL BEFORE *ANY* OF THEM WAKE UP, THOUGH.

The crone fixed her bright black eyes on Harriet, who had a feeling that she was missing something. (The trouble with witches is that they are much like a certain kind of teacher, and they won't tell you the answer to a question if they believe you're capable of working it out on your own.)

"I'll have to convince him to kiss all the newts too, I guess," said Harriet. She didn't mind the hunting newts herself, who were generally good-natured and liked having their gill-slits scratched, but a stuck-up prince might certainly balk at kissing a newt.

WHERE AM I GONNA FIND A PRINCE LIKE THAT? PARTICULARLY NOW THAT I'M NOT INVINCIBLE ANYMORE!

I HAVE TOTAL FAITH IN YOU, MY DEAR. INVINCIBILITY ISN'T EVERYTHING.

YEAH, BUT IT'S A *LOT.*

"Just remember," said the crone, "magic has a *long tail*." And she gave Harriet another very hard look.

"Err?" said Harriet, glancing back at her own tiny, stubby tail. "If you say so?" She wasn't sure what the crone was talking about, but the way that she emphasized the words meant that they were important.

That was the trouble with witches, they expected you to be smarter than you really were.

The crone shook her head, sitting back. "Just remember that, will you? And now, I might be able to give you some help . . ." She went into the back of the cottage and began banging around in a closet. "Now, where did I put that thing . . . ?"

Harriet relaxed back into the chair and had another cookie. If the Crone of the Blighted Waste had some enchanted object to help her, she was in a much better state. Maybe it would be a magic sword. You could do a lot with a magic sword. Or a cloak of invisibility.

HMM, I COULD SNEAK INTO A CASTLE IN THE INVISIBLE CLOAK, FIND A PRINCE, HIT HIM OVER THE HEAD, TIE HIM TO MUMFREY, AND BY THE TIME HE WOKE UP, WE'D BE HALFWAY HOME . . .

"Right!" said the crone, emerging from the back with dust on her apron. "Found it!" She held out her hand.

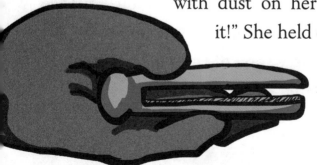

...IT'S A CLOTHESPIN.

A MAGIC CLOTHESPIN OF BINDING!

I AM NOT GETTING PAST THE BIT WHERE IT'S A *CLOTHESPIN.*

"Snap this clothespin on anyone or anything, and it'll stay snapped," said the crone. "It's really very useful."

"If you're trying to do laundry in a high wind, I suppose," said Harriet dubiously. "I don't suppose you've got a magic sword or anything back there?"

"It's the clothespin or nothing," said the crone firmly.

Harriet sighed. However, she had not spent the last two years traveling the world for nothing. She knew that if a witch gives you something, the odds are good that when you are in some dire peril, it will be exactly the thing you need.

Anyway, she still had a perfectly good un-enchanted sword.

"Thank you," she said, putting the clothespin in her pocket. "I'm sure it will come in handy."

"You're not sure of anything of the sort," said the crone cheerfully, "but you've learned to be polite to people who can turn you into a turnip, and that's not a bad skill." She handed Harriet a small sack. "Here are some cookies for the road, and a bottle of antiseptic. You put that on your scratches morning and evening, and I don't want any complaining about it stinging. I shall be watching you in my scrying mirror to make sure." (Many witches have scrying mirrors, which allow them to see what is going on in distant places. The Crone of the Blighted Waste kept hers in the spare bedroom, which was very surprising to guests who would go to check their hair and suddenly have a view of India or Samarkand.)

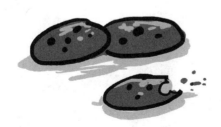

And so, the valiant princess Harriet took her cookies and her enchanted clothespin and her un-enchanted sword and climbed onto Mumfrey's back to set off in search of a prince.

CHAPTER 15

The first palace that Harriet came to was very tall, with banners flying from the tops of the towers. It had a charming moat, blue slate roof tiles, and was in every way a perfect castle.

Princess Harriet rode up the winding road to the castle door, climbed off Mumfrey's back, and knocked.

The door opened immediately, and a butler looked down his nose at Harriet. He was tall and thin and haughty and looked as if he had coat-hangers for bones.

"You and everyone else," said the butler. "What is your name?"

"Princess Harriet."

The butler's face did not move at all, but his eyes definitely flickered a bit. "I will go and see if the prince is available."

AREN'T YOU GOING TO ASK ME IN?

NO.

SLAM!

"I have half a mind to ride away and go find another prince," she told Mumfrey. "But Mom and Dad need help."

The butler returned a few minutes later and said, "The prince is not at home."

"I can wait," said Harriet, shoving her foot in the door.

"No," said the butler, "you can't. The prince is not at home. He will not be home for the foreseeable future. As far as *you* are concerned, Princess, he will never be at home again."

Harriet's jaw dropped at the sheer rudeness of this, and the butler took advantage of her astonishment to slide her foot off the threshold and slam the door again.

HOW DARE—

OF ALL THE—

WHEN I'M QUEEN,
I'M CONQUERING THIS STUPID
CASTLE AND TURNING IT INTO A
HOME FOR SICK NEWTS!

"Qwerk!" said Mumfrey, and left a steaming pile of quail poop on the doorstep of the perfect castle.

The next palace was even larger, and according to a helpful peasant on the road, had not one but *two* princes in residence. Harriet felt much more optimistic.

It was just as perfect as the last one. The road was lined with topiary, which is an art form where people cut bushes into the shapes of animals. A row of enormous boxwood rabbits watched Harriet ride up to the door.

The butler who opened this door was nearly identical to the first butler, except that he was even taller and thinner and more haughty-looking. He looked like a coatrack wearing a suit.

"I'm looking for a prince," said Harriet. "Either one. It's an emergency."

"It always is," said the butler sourly, and slammed the door.

The door opened again, and the butler said, "What's your name?"

"Princess Harriet," said Harriet.

"*You're* a princess?" said the butler.

"Absolutely," said Harriet, trying to look pale and melancholy and as if she were capable of balancing a book on her head.

"Wait here," said the butler, and slammed the door again.

Another few moments slid by, and the butler came back. "*Harriet*, you say? Harriet *Hamsterbone*, by chance?"

"Uh-huh," said Harriet. "And you don't have to slam the door. You can just shut it. It's cool."

The butler did not scowl—she suspected that his face could not move that much—but the air around him gave the impression of scowling anyway. When he shut the door this time, without slamming it, Harriet heard a whisper of conversation from behind the door.

YOU KNOW, IF I WERE STILL INVINCIBLE, I'D STORM THIS CASTLE AND *MAKE* THE PRINCE COME BACK WITH ME.

The door opened again. The butler started to say something, and somebody behind him whispered, *"That's* Crazy Princess Hamsterbone? Really?"

"Really," said Harriet grimly. "And I need a prince. My family's under a spell, and I need a prince to break it."

"His Grace is not at home," said the butler.

"What about the other prince?"

"His other Grace is also not at home."

"I thought she'd have, like, fangs!" said one of the princes.

The other prince giggled.

"No one is at home," said the butler, very forcefully, and slammed the door.

Harriet turned around, walked back down the road—Mumfrey followed, qwerking nervously—and she proceeded to decapitate every single topiary rabbit she saw, as well as a topiary lungfish and a pair of topiary parakeets.

"Qwerk-qwerk?" asked Mumfrey, which is Quail for "Do you feel better now?"

Harriet put her arms around Mumfrey's neck and pressed her face into his feathers. This alarmed Mumfrey a great deal, because Harriet generally required comforting about as much as a steel bear trap does, which is to say, not very often.

Harriet felt awful. She couldn't help but think that if she were a more princessly princess—the sort who was pale and melancholy and didn't stomp—the princes would have helped her instead of leaving her on the doorstep, and her family might even now be waking up.

She had spent all this time thinking that Prince Cecil was awful. Now it was starting to look like he was the best prince that her parents had been able to get.

She took a deep breath. She wasn't crying, exactly. She was just . . . breathing hard. With a little bit of a catch in it. Yeah. She'd fought ogres. No stupid princes who hid behind their butlers were going to make *her* cry.

Fangs. Hmmph. Harriet wished she did have fangs. She'd bite that prince's stupid ears off, and make him *eat* them. Without salt.

"All right," she said to Mumfrey, cleaning sap and bits of bark off her sword. "This isn't going well. We'll try one more, and if their prince isn't at home, invincible or not, I'm storming the castle."

CHAPTER 16

The third castle did not look nearly as perfect as the other two. It was large and ramshackle and the moat had green gunk in it and a sign that said "No Fishing." The drawbridge did not seem to work anymore, and had broken down about six inches off the ground, so Mumfrey had to hop up onto it to get to the castle door. There were no flying banners, and a bird had nested on one of the roofs.

Harriet had spent most of the ride over wondering gloomily if she should pretend to be a more princessly princess, and had finally decided that it was probably a bad idea. She'd need better clothes. And anyway, a really princessly princess would never have thrown Ratshade into the enchanted wheel in the first place, so the act would have been over once she started explaining why she needed a prince's help.

She got down from Mumfrey's back and knocked on the door. Her stomach felt all woogly, like when she had to go to the dentist.

CAN I HELP YOU?

Harriet was relieved that the woman who answered the door wasn't a butler who looked like a coatrack. "I'm looking for a prince!" she blurted out.

The woman sighed. "Aren't we all, honey, aren't we all . . . ?" She dried her hands on her apron.

"It's not for me," said Harriet. "My parents are under a curse. Only a prince can break it."

"Oh, honey," said the matronly hamster kindly, "I'm afraid you're too late. The prince—well, he's under a curse too."

"Really?" said Harriet, surprised. She'd thought that curses were rarer than that.

"He's at the top of a glass mountain," said the other hamster. "Guarded by a fearsome hydra with five heads. I thought the hydra was a bit excessive, because no one's ever even made it up the glass mountain, but there you are."

MAYBE I CAN HELP.
I'VE GOT SOME EXPERIENCE
WITH BREAKING CURSES.

WHAT'S YOUR NAME?

... PRINCESS
HARRIET HAMSTERBONE.

CRAZY PRINCESS HAMSTERBONE?

... YES.

THAT'S **WONDERFUL!** YOU'RE JUST THE PERSON WE NEED!

"Really?" asked Harriet as the matronly hamster pulled her inside the castle and beckoned to Mumfrey to follow. The quail stepped daintily into the foyer and tried not to knock anything over.

"Absolutely!" said her hostess. "When I heard about you, I thought—now there's a princess who might be able to help my son!"

"Your son?" asked Harriet, trying to keep up with the conversation.

"Well, yes," said the other hamster. "I'm the queen."

CHAPTER 17

Harriet was not used to a queen that roamed around the castle in an apron, looking like a housekeeper, but it soon became obvious that this was not the sort of castle she was used to.

It was . . . well . . . *shabby*. The furniture was old and worn and had been gnawed on by countless generations of hamster toddlers (and a hamster just getting in his adult chisel teeth can really gnaw. Some of the legs had been reinforced with sheet metal). The tapestries were pretty but threadbare, and there weren't servants and guards every few feet.

"Not too many of us here," said the queen over her shoulder. "Just me and the gardeners and two maids and Cook. And we've got a master-at-arms somewhere, but I don't like to bother him when he's napping."

Harriet didn't mind at all. It was refreshing to go somewhere where you weren't constantly being dusted around and swept around and curtseyed at. Her mother would have been horrified.

"So, Your Majesty, about this curse . . ." she said as they walked through the great hall, and Mumfrey padded along behind them.

OH PLEASE, NOT "YOUR MAJESTY." I'M HAZEL.

... ERR, QUEEN HAZEL, THEN— ISN'T IT USUALLY PRINCESSES THAT GET CURSED?

WELL, YES. THERE WAS A BIT OF A MIX-UP THERE.

"You see," said Queen Hazel, taking Mumfrey and Harriet past the hall and into a small drawing room off to one side, "we've never been a very wealthy kingdom. And so poor Prince Wilbur was wearing a hand-me-down christening gown from his cousin Matilda, and I'm afraid it was rather pink. So when the wicked fairy showed up, she thought he was a princess, and . . . well . . ."

"At any rate," said Queen Hazel, "we've heard all the stories about how wonderfully you handled those ogres! You're just the sort of princess we need! Someone who can give that hydra a proper whomping! And—err—well, whatever you do to teach a glass mountain who's boss . . ." She waved a hand, presumably in the direction of the glass mountain. "I've got a map—it's only a day or two away, you can't miss it. And we'll pack a lunch for you and your quail."

And so, before she even had time to think, Princess Harriet was back on the road, in pursuit of a prince at the top of a fabulous glass mountain.

CHAPTER 18

The glass mountain was easy to find. In the daylight, it glittered like diamonds.

Princess Harriet had never actually climbed a glass mountain before, but she had an idea. It was extremely obvious, but presumably the previous people who had tried to climb the glass mountain hadn't been trying very hard.

As for the hydra, she was a little more worried. She'd fought a hydra once, and it wasn't easy. When you chop off one of a hydra's heads, it immediately grows two more heads. A little indiscriminate chopping, and suddenly your five-headed hydra has eighty-nine heads and a real attitude problem. You can theoretically stop this by burning each stump with a torch, but it's very messy, to say nothing of the difficulty of carrying a torch in one hand and a sword in the other and trying to use both on a giant dragony thing that's trying to bite you.

Harriet had come out of the last fight covered in bald patches where she'd burned her own fur off by accident, and Mumfrey hadn't stopped snickering for a month.

THIS WOULD BE A LOT EASIER IF I WAS STILL INVINCIBLE.

They reached the
glass mountain a
little after dawn.

"Hmm," said
Harriet.

She climbed down from Mumfrey's back and went up to the mountain. She poked it a few times.

Definitely glass. The surface of the mountain was as smooth as a punchbowl. There was no question of climbing it. Anything but a fly would slide right off. She rapped her knuckles on it, and it went "tink."

"Right!" Harriet dusted her hands together and got back on Mumfrey. "I have a plan."

"Qwerk."

"It may even be a brilliant plan."

"Qwerk?"

"You're going to hate it."

They backtracked to the nearest village. The village was called Brickingham and it held an annual cabbage festival. The only other significant thing about Brickingham, so far as Princess Harriet was concerned, was that it had a hardware store.

At the hardware store, she bought two toilet plungers, eight bungee cords, and a hacksaw.

They rode back to the glass mountain. Harriet set to work.

First she used the hacksaw to cut off the wooden handles of the plungers, because it is very hard to chop through wood with a sword, and the sword tends to be useless for brandishing at monsters afterward. When she was left with four large rubber plunger heads, she picked up a handful of bungee cords and turned to Mumfrey.

QWEEERRRRKKK . . . ?

"I told you that you were going to hate it," said Harriet.

Mumfrey hid his head under his wing, and refused to come out while Harriet strapped the plunger heads to his feet and tied them in place with the bungee cords.

"There!" said Harriet, sitting back in satisfaction. "Now we can get up that stupid mountain!"

It took some coaxing, but Mumfrey was eventually persuaded to come out from under his wing and test his new shoes.

He took a wobbly step along the ground, then another one. Then he reached the base of the mountain, and put a foot up on it.

The plunger heads—which were really giant suction cups, when you got right down to it—stuck firmly to the glass.

Mumfrey stared at his foot in astonishment. He put his other foot on the glass, and it stuck. He lifted the first foot—it took a bit of effort and made a loud *SKWTHUP!* sound—and put it down farther up the glass.

"Yeeeehaaa!" cried Harriet, and vaulted onto the quail's back. "Let's go!"

CHAPTER 19

It took about half an hour to reach the top of the glass mountain. Mumfrey had to spread his wings occasionally and flap for balance—he was too big to fly, but he could still flap—but the suction cups worked wonderfully. All Harriet had to do was hold on and enjoy the ride.

They reached the top. It wasn't very big. There was a small cottage at the top, and in front of it, looking very bored, a hamster and a hydra were playing cards.

"Whoa!" said the hamster, staring at her. "Did you really manage to climb the mountain?"

"Nothing to it," said Harriet. "Are you Prince Wilbur?" The other hamster looked to be about her own age.

"That's me. I've got a crown around here somewhere..."

ERR...
HAVE YOU COME
TO RESCUE ME?

"That's the plan," said Harriet, drawing her sword.

The hydra hissed and dropped its cards. Harriet took a step forward.

"Qweerrgg," said Mumfrey, which was Quail for "I'm going to sit this one out, my feet are tired."

A head darted at her, jaws snapping. Harriet slapped it away with the flat of her sword, careful not to cut the beast, for fear of spawning another head.

The princess gritted her teeth. Why hadn't she brought torches? What was a little burned fur, really? It grew back eventually! She was going to have to try to knock it out with her sword hilt, which is a lot harder when there are five separate heads you have to whack.

Wilbur stepped hurriedly in front of the hydra. "No! Wait! Don't hurt Heady!"

YOU *NAMED* THE *HYDRA*.

SO? I BET YOU NAMED YOUR QUAIL!

THAT'S DIFFERENT!

"Look," said Wilbur, "I've been up here for months. Since my twelfth birthday. Heady and I play cards. She's really nice. And she bakes great cookies!"

The hydra blushed and tried to look modest.

Harriet rubbed her face. "Okay. Well, I've got no beef with Heady . . . I just need a prince."

Wilbur narrowed his eyes. "You don't want to marry me, do you? Because I'm really not interested in getting married. I'm sure you're a very nice princess—"

"Ha!" said Harriet.

"—but I'm twelve."

IT'S COOL. I'M TWELVE TOO. BELIEVE ME, I AM IN *NO* HURRY TO GET MARRIED.

"I need you to break a curse," Harriet said.

"Oh. Is that all?" Prince Wilbur relaxed. "Of course I'll help! Curses are no fun. What do I need to do?"

"There's this magic sleep, and the only thing that can break it is a prince's kiss."

LOOK,
I JUST TOLD YOU, I'M NOT
INTERESTED—

NOT ME!
MY MOM AND DAD!

YOU WANT ME
TO KISS YOUR *MOM
AND DAD?*

"And everyone else in the palace," said Harriet. "There's a hundred and seventeen of them."

"You know, if it's all the same to you, I'll stay here with Heady," said Prince Wilbur. "There is entirely too much kissing involved in this curse." He made a face.

"It's *not* all the same to me," said Harriet. "You're the last prince I've got. The others all laughed at me or made their butlers tell me they weren't at home. They wouldn't even listen about the curse."

"That was pretty awful of them," said Wilbur sympathetically. "They're not very nice princes, though. They won't talk to me either, because we're poor."

"Yeah. And your mom—the queen—asked me to come and get you off this mountain."

"Oh, Mom . . ." Wilbur sighed. "I hope she's okay. What's your name, anyway?"

Harriet sighed. "Princess Harriet."

"You mean—"

YES, YES!
*CRAZY PRINCESS
HAMSTERBONE!*
HAPPY?!

There was a brief silence. Harriet's face felt hot.

Wilbur scuffed a toe along the glass and said, "I always thought you sounded awesome."

Harriet blinked.

"You got to have such cool adventures. You fought ogres! And jousted! And they say you dove off the Cliffs of Perdition, which are like eight hundred feet high!"

"Nine hundred twenty-three," mumbled Harriet, staring at her feet.

"I always wanted to do that kinda thing," said Wilbur. "But it never happened. I mean, we couldn't afford a riding quail or anything. And I had to get a paper route so we could afford to fix the castle roof. So I never did get to have any adventures."

Harriet felt as if she had been carrying around a heavy rock, and someone had just told her that she could finally set it down. She reached out and took Wilbur's hand.

"Well," she said, "now you get to have one."

CHAPTER 20

The trip back to Harriet's kingdom took a lot longer than Harriet was expecting.

It wasn't that anyone tried to stop them. Bandits would occasionally try to hassle a hamster girl with a sword, but *nobody* was going to mess with a hamster riding a hydra. On at least one occasion, thugs jumped out of the woods, took one look at them, apologized, and asked if they knew the way to the cabbage festival.

No, the problem was that Prince Wilbur just wasn't used to adventures.

He tried. He really did. Harriet tried to be patient, because she knew he was trying, but she still occasionally wanted to dump him off a cliff for being useless.

Where Harriet had spent the last two years pretty much living in Mumfrey's saddle, Wilbur could only ride Heady for a few hours before he needed a break.

SO ... SORE ...

Harriet bought a few goosedown pillows at the nearest town, and they tried to pad the saddle. It helped, even if it looked ridiculous.

Heady was a surprisingly good cook, so there were no problems with the quality of the food—although Harriet never got used to seeing the hydra scramble an egg with a whisk in one set of teeth and the frying pan in another—but camp at night was tough too.

"We may have been poor," grumbled Wilbur, "but we always had *beds*."

"You get used to it," said Harriet.

Keeping her temper had never been one of Harriet's strong suits, but she gritted her teeth and tried not to scream. It wasn't his fault. She hadn't been very good at the adventuring life at first either. Her first week, she'd been so bad at cooking that she had to share Mumfrey's birdseed a couple of times.

Wilbur was trying. He didn't mean to whine. She kept telling herself that.

And he was . . . well, to give Wilbur credit, he was *nice*. When someone saw Heady and screamed and ran away, he would spend hours consoling the poor hydra and telling her that people just needed to learn to see the beauty inside. Harriet couldn't have told anybody that, at least not with a straight face.

Other than being screamed at by the occasional terrified citizen, Heady was thrilled to be out. She hadn't been off the glass mountain in ages, and was excited to see the world. She and Mumfrey had struck up a friendship, based largely on comparing how bony their respective rider's rear ends were.

The princess had other problems too. She kept worrying that something was going to get into the castle, past the thorns, and get her parents. What if somebody decided to take over the kingdom? Sure, they'd need a couple dozen men with axes, but that wasn't hard to come by, was it?

Her mom and dad didn't need to eat or drink in their enchanted sleep, but what if something else went wrong?

"They'll be fine," said Wilbur. "My mom always says that things look darkest just before the dawn."

"Unless you're underground," said Harriet. "Or at the bottom of a dungeon. Then it doesn't matter what time it is."

" . . . um," said Wilbur.

CHAPTER 21

When they finally reached the top of the hill leading to the castle, Harriet's relief was so intense she nearly cried. The brambles were still in place around the castle. Nobody had gotten in.

Actually, they were more than "in place." When Harriet tried to find the tunnel she'd hacked out, it was so overgrown that she could barely see where it had been. If she hadn't left an ax sticking out of a briar trunk at the entryway, she might never have found it again.

"I don't *think* you have to kiss the brambles," said Harriet. "Although . . . could you try? I mean, one little kiss is bound to be easier than hacking our way back through there . . ."

I'D RATHER HACK.

Harriet handed Wilbur the ax.

He lasted about five minutes before dropping the ax and planting a smooch on the nearest briar.

Nothing happened.

Both of them muttered bad words under their

breath. Harriet's was much better, but then again, she'd learned it from a one-legged weasel pirate on the Seas of Terror, and they have much better bad words than you are likely to learn on a paper route.

They went back to chopping brambles.

Harriet took over as soon as Wilbur's arms were tired—about five minutes—and started breaking the job up into fractions.

OKAY...
FIGURE I'VE DONE ABOUT A TENTH... IF I GET THAT BRANCH THERE AND THAT ONE THERE, THAT'S ANOTHER TENTH, WHICH IS A FIFTH...CLEAR OUT THAT BIT THERE AND CALL IT A FOURTH...

This did not get the brambles chopped any faster, but it did make things seem less daunting.

It was nearly nightfall by the time they reached the stableyard. Mumfrey rushed in to check on the other quail. They were all still fast asleep in the stables.

Ratshade was still sleeping as well. The only thing that had changed was the pile of wood left by the enchanted hamster wheel, which had turned into a pile of black ash.

That . . . and Ratshade's nails.

"Yeesh!" said Wilbur, staring down at the sleeping fairy. "What's with her nails?"

"They must grow really fast," said Harriet. "Wow."

"Poor rat. That must be really uncomfortable."

Harriet gave him a look. "You know she's the one who cursed everybody, right?"

"Oh. Hmm. How do you suppose she goes to the bathroom?" asked Wilbur.

"Very carefully."

C'MON, LET'S GET TO THE GREAT HALL.

CHAPTER 22

Prince Wilbur kissed everyone.

He kissed the quail in their stalls and the newts in their kennels. He kissed the dukes and the earls and the viscounts and the regular count. He kissed the servants and the guards and the pages and the cook and the maids.

At first he was squeamish and would have to screw up his courage to kiss a sleeping hamster on the ear or the cheek, but after about forty kisses, he stopped caring and started complaining.

"They're not waking up, though," said the prince, kissing Harriet's mother on the cheek and her father (awkwardly) on top of his head. "And I'm starting to feel really weird about this."

"They won't wake up until you've kissed everybody," said Harriet. "The Crone of the Blighted Waste told me so. You're doing great."

Wilbur sighed.

The day wore on. He kissed the two pages in the boys' bathroom and the six guards in the tower bedroom and a couple of visiting dignitaries and the castle janitor and the three stablehands tending the quail. (Mumfrey watched, very concerned, as he kissed the various quail. Those were his friends, after all!)

He stopped occasionally to take a drink of water. Harriet watched impatiently.

He kissed another newt sleeping in front of the fire, and turned finally to Prince Cecil, who was still asleep at the bottom of the stairs.

"He should be the last one!" said Harriet enthusiastically.

"I can't feel my face."

"It's probably better that way. Do you *want* to feel this?"

"Not ... really ..." He frowned. "Did this poor guy fall down the stairs?"

UM. SURE. THAT'S PROBABLY WHAT HAPPENED.

Harriet quivered with excitement. Wilbur screwed up his face—the other prince had drooled in his sleep, and it was all very unpleasant—and kissed the tip of the prince's ear.

Nothing happened.

"Give it a minute," said Harriet.

A minute passed. Nothing continued to happen.

"Please don't tell me I've kissed all those people for nothing," said Wilbur. "My lips feel like old tires, and I'm still not entirely sure there isn't something deeply creepy about all this."

"They're supposed to wake up!" said Harriet. "The crone said! She said once you'd kissed everyone, they'd all wake up!" She put her hands on her hips.

YOU MUST HAVE MISSED SOMEONE. ARE YOU SURE YOU KISSED ALL THE NEWTS?

"I think I kissed some of those newts twice," said Wilbur.

"And the dukes and the earls and the viscounts?"

"Check, check, and check."

"And I *know* you kissed my mom and dad . . ."

"I would prefer not to dwell on that, thank you."

Harriet bit her lip. The crone had said that the prince had to kiss everyone in the palace who had fallen asleep, and then everyone would wake up. What was she missing?

"Everyone in the palace . . ." she muttered. "Everyone in the palace . . ."

The crone had even given her a *look*. What had the look meant?

And then it hit her.

OH, *NO.*
WE FORGOT ABOUT
RATSHADE!

CHAPTER 23

"But I don't *want* to kiss an evil fairy!" said Wilbur, for about the eight hundredth time.

"We don't have a choice," said Harriet, tightening a rope around Ratshade's left foot. "We're going to have to wake her up. We'll just have to make sure she can't escape."

"But . . . it's not that I don't want to help . . . I mean, I'd feel awful if it was *my* mom under a magic sleep . . ."

"Look," said Harriet, "if you don't kiss Ratshade, then all the other kisses won't work. And you'll have kissed the newts and Prince Cecil and my parents for nothing."

I SUPPOSE WHEN YOU PUT IT LIKE *THAT* . . .

Harriet pulled the last belt tight and stood back to survey her handiwork. "There. If she can escape this . . . well . . ."

The truth was that if Ratshade could escape from the pile of ropes, belts, stakes, weights, and handcuffs that Harriet had shackled her with, there was really nothing that they could do about it.

"That's everything I can think of to do," Harriet said. "Are we all ready?"

"Hiss!"

"Qwerk!"

". . . I guess."

The princess drew her sword and nodded to Wilbur.

Wilbur gulped and slowly bent down toward

Ratshade. Kissing evil fairies had not been in the job description.

The same cold wind that had struck Harriet before came shrieking out of nowhere. It whipped Mumfrey's feathers and tangled Heady's heads and blew Harriet's whiskers sideways.

This time, though, the wind seemed to be coming from behind them, and blowing directly *into* the body of Ratshade.

The wind shrieked.

The pile of belts and ropes binding Ratshade creaked warningly. Buckles rattled as it vibrated and shook. Heady grabbed Wilbur's shirt in one

set of teeth and tried to pull him away from the wicked fairy and her bindings.

And then, just as it had before, the wind whipped around them one last time and faded into silence.

"Did . . . did it work?" asked Wilbur. "Is she awake?"

"I'm not sure," said Harriet.

The pile of ropes exploded.

"Yes," snarled Ratshade, spitting out the last words of a spell that made the ropes whip off her like frightened snakes. "I'm awake."

CHAPTER 24

Harriet was feeling a relief so intense that her knees were getting a bit shaky.

The spell had been broken! Prince Wilbur's kiss had worked! Ratshade was awake, and that meant that everybody else would be waking up too, including her parents!

There *was* the small matter of the angry fairy and the bit where Harriet herself was probably about to be turned into a turnip or a sea cucumber or something equally unfortunate, but these things happened.

Ratshade pointed a shaking finger at Harriet.
Her claws had grown so rapidly in her sleep that
it looked as if she had earthworms strapped to
the ends.

Harriet gripped her sword more tightly and took a step forward.

Ratshade sneered at her. "Still playing with swords? You should learn how to act like a princess!" She twitched her claws, and the sword shot out of Harriet's hands and buried itself in the wall next to Wilbur's head. Wilbur yelped and jumped sideways.

"I *am* acting like a princess!" yelled Harriet. "I'm a princess, and therefore any way that I act—oh, never mind!" She lunged for the sword.

Ratshade's spell hit her before she made it ten feet. It felt like somebody had clubbed her in the back of her knees.

OOF!

Ratshade raised both hands and whipped them through the air like a conductor.

HISS!

...HISSS?

Two of Heady's heads crashed together, two more tied themselves in a knot, and the fifth head looked extremely confused.

With all the heads out of commission, Heady could no longer see where she was going and fell over on her side. Ratshade snickered.

The quail lunged. His topknot quivered with rage, and the spurs on his scaly feet glittered.

She rolled her eyes, stuck out an arm, and Mumfrey's feet stopped moving. The rest of Mumfrey did *not* stop moving, which meant that he went beak-first into the dirt.

Wilbur looked at Heady, looked at Mumfrey, looked at Harriet, who was still crawling grimly toward her sword—and finally looked at Ratshade.

The wicked fairy was a terrifying sight. Ash streaked her fur and her eyes glittered as red as dying suns. The stump of her tail twitched back and forth like a metronome. Her claws seemed to writhe as she lifted her hands.

"A prince!" hissed Ratshade. "A prince has come to fight me!?" Static sparked and crackled over her fur. "Princesses are nothing, but a prince . . . !"

It would be nice to report that Wilbur said something heroic at this juncture, something really impressive and clever and suited to a fairy-tale prince. But it can be hard to think of clever and impressive things to say when you are facing a profoundly wicked fairy, particularly when you aren't used to adventures.

Harriet sighed.

"Not much of a prince, are you?" growled Rat-shade. "Well, she's not much of a princess, so I suppose that fits. But you did break my curse . . ."

She raised her claws over her head and strode forward.

Wilbur looked around wildly, and saw the sword.

No! Harriet wanted to yell as Wilbur yanked the sword out of the wall. *No, you idiot, you're holding it all wrong, you don't know the first thing about using a sword, you're going to cut your own leg off—*

But she didn't, because Ratshade was ignoring her, and had walked right by her, and Harriet didn't want to draw her attention. Apparently the wicked fairy didn't think that princesses were worth worrying about. It didn't matter that Harriet had thrown her into the hamster wheel earlier—in Ratshade's world, princesses existed to be cursed and weren't good for much else.

I'll show her. I'll figure out a way . . .

For some reason, she couldn't look away from the stump of Ratshade's tail. It twitched in front of her, as if something was still attached to it . . . back and forth . . .

. . . back and forth . . .

Magic has a very long tail, the crone had said.

"A sword?" sneered Ratshade. "Fool! Do you really think you can hurt me with that? Blades cannot cut me!"

Since Harriet's plan had mostly relied on having a sword, this was unwelcome news.

I'd chop her tail off, if I could! And if she still . . . had one . . .

. . . what if she does?

"I don't have to," said Wilbur, and drawing his arm back, he threw the sword across the space between them.

"Ha!" said Ratshade. "You missed!"

"I," said Prince Wilbur with great dignity, "am a paper boy. I *never* miss."

Ratshade turned.

CHAPTER 25

Ratshade opened her mouth to say something—an insult, a magic phrase, Harriet had no idea and wasn't about to give her the chance. The hamster princess swung the sword up over her head and down in a great cleaving arc.

She wasn't aiming at Ratshade, though—not exactly. Many wicked fairies are indeed immune to blades, unless you have a magic sword forged of moonlight and iron, and those are expensive even for princesses. Harriet's sword was plain

steel and probably would have bounced right off
Ratshade.

Instead, Harriet aimed for the stump
of Ratshade's tail.

*Crone, I hope you knew
what you were talking
about!*

NNNNN

NNOOOOOOOOOOO!!!

The blade passed so close to the wicked fairy that her ash-streaked fur rippled with it, and chopped through the air a millimeter away.

Ratshade screamed.

It's not widely known, but when a rat trades its tail for magic, the magic attached itself to the stump in the same way that the tail did.

Princess Harriet had just amputated Ratshade's magic.

Electricity sparked and whined through the air. Harriet's sword turned red-hot and the hamster princess dropped it, where it promptly melted into a small molten puddle.

"Whoa," said Harriet.

"My magic!" screamed Ratshade.

She was still a wicked fairy—being a fairy is something you're born with, and nobody can take that away—but she was suddenly much less powerful. She spun around and tried to cast a spell that would have blasted Harriet into smithereens—and nothing happened.

MISSING SOMETHING?

Harriet had no idea what Ratshade would try next. She hadn't been sure that chopping off Ratshade's tail would even work. That had been her only sword, and unless she could grab a broom from the stable, she was completely out of weapons.

She was, however, a bit surprised when Ratshade decided to try and strangle her.

"I'll kill you!" screamed the evil rat fairy. "I'll turn you into cufflinks—into a raindrop—into a six-note kazoo solo!"

Harriet pried at the fingers around her throat. Ratshade's monstrous claws were cutting into her skin and making it hard to breathe, and she had absolutely no desire to be turned into a kazoo solo.

The rat was bigger than she was, and hideously strong. She dropped one hand and began fumbling around for something—a rock, a broom, anything—to whack Ratshade over the head with.

"No, you aren't!" shrieked Ratshade. "A *proper* princess would *die!*"

She couldn't breathe. Bright spots were starting to form in front of her eyes. But Harriet's questing hand landed in her pocket, and found something she'd completely forgotten.

The clothespin.

With her last strength, she whipped the clothespin out of her pocket and snapped it shut on Ratshade's twitching nose.

The world went gray.

Suddenly she could breathe again. The claws were gone. Harriet pulled herself up on her elbows and watched as Ratshade staggered around the stableyard, clawing at the clothespin.

Either the magic of the Clothespin of Binding was such that it wouldn't come off Ratshade's nose, or the wicked fairy's claws had simply grown too long for her to be able to get a grip on it.

Her flailing brought her too near Mumfrey. Even with his eyes crossed from having hit his beak too hard, the quail managed to stick out a wing. Ratshade tumbled over it and landed on her back.

"Enough!" she cried (although with the clothespin on her nose, it came out as "Ennogggk!"). She waved her hands in the air, and with the last of her fairy strength, she vanished.

Harriet sat up and rubbed her neck.

"Is...is it over?" asked Wilbur. He had prudently taken refuge behind a haystack. "Is she gone?"

"I think she's gone," croaked Harriet. Her throat was sore and raspy. "We'll have to check with the crone, but I don't think she'll come back unless she can get the clothespin off."

"Oh good," said Wilbur. "In that case, I think I'm going to faint."

And he did.

Harriet rolled her eyes.

CHAPTER 26

The days that followed were busy. Harriet had to explain everything to her parents and to everyone in the palace, and then she had to explain it all over again three or four times, because no one was listening and everybody was saying things like "*How long* were we asleep?" and "Are you *quite sure* Ratshade is gone?" and "Where did that smashed-up hamster wheel in the stableyard come from?"

WE CAN'T POSSIBLY HAVE BEEN ASLEEP THAT LONG. I KNOW IT PROBABLY SEEMED LIKE A LONG TIME TO *YOU*, PRINCESS—

OH, GIVE IT A REST.

There was also the matter of the brambles, which had not vanished when everyone woke up. The royal gardeners were out hacking at stems and trunks and vines for days, and the royal guard and the royal woodcutters had to get involved too. Harriet's father spent a lot of time wandering around the castle muttering about the foundations.

IF I EVER FIND THAT MIDDLE FAIRY GOD-MOUSE, I'M GOING TO SUE!

There was also the problem of Harriet's mother and Wilbur. The queen had accepted, somewhat reluctantly, that Prince Cecil had not saved the day (possibly because he'd still been asleep when she woke up), so instead she had glommed onto Wilbur.

SO YOU'LL BE GETTING MARRIED NOW?

Still, it was very difficult to tell the queen anything she didn't want to hear. Harriet had apparently inherited her stubbornness from her mother.

"You have to marry the prince that saved you!" the queen said. "Otherwise why would princes save anybody?"

"Because they're decent people," grumbled Harriet.

The king had already given Wilbur a large cash reward for his services, which Wilbur had dutifully sent back home to help fix up his mother's castle, but the hamster queen couldn't seem to get past the fact that Wilbur was a prince, and princesses married princes, and that was just the way the world worked.

She'd also started talking about deportment lessons again.

"Keep it quiet," Harriet told Mumfrey as she saddled him up. "I'm getting out of here before someone tries to balance a book on my head. I hear there's an ogre up in North Hamworth that hasn't converted to vegetarianism yet."

"Qwerk," said Mumfrey very quietly.

"Escaping!" said Wilbur. "Your mom scares me! I meant to go back home right away, but she kept insisting I stay longer!"

"Tell me about it," said Harriet. She swung up onto Mumfrey's back. Heady hissed at them in a friendly fashion. The hydra was loaded with pillows.

They slipped out of the stableyard and onto the road. Wilbur fiddled with the reins.

SO ... UM ... I WAS WONDERING ... I MEAN, IT WAS SCARY, BUT THE ADVENTURE *WAS* KIND OF COOL ...

YOU COMPLAINED ABOUT SLEEPING ON THE GROUND THE *WHOLE* TIME.

IT'LL BE FINE! I TOOK PART OF MY REWARD IN PILLOWS!

FINE, FINE . . .

I'M GOING TO GO SLAY AN OGRE. YOU WANT TO COME WITH? WE CAN STOP BY YOUR PLACE FIRST.

YEAH!

DON'T MISS THESE OTHER
URSULA

ABOUT the AUTHOR

Ursula Vernon (www.ursulavernon.com) is an award-winning author and illustrator whose work has won a Hugo Award and been nominated for an Eisner. She loves birding, gardening, and spunky heroines. She is the first to admit that she would make a terrible princess.